This book belongs to

_A Ma_

Mohammed

First published by Parragon in 2012
Parragon
Queen Street House
4 Queen Street
Bath BA1 1HE, UK
www.parragon.com

Edited by: Gemma Lowe   Production by: Emma Fulleylove

ISBN 978-1-4454-4777-3

Printed in China

Disney · PIXAR
BRAVE

Adapted by Elle D. Risco

Illustrated by Studio IBOIX and Maria Elena Naggi
and the Disney Storybook Artists

Bath · New York · Singapore · Hong Kong · Cologne · Delhi
Melbourne · Amsterdam · Johannesburg · Auckland · Shenzhen

Long ago, in the Scottish Highlands, there was a kingdom called DunBroch. The land was ruled by King Fergus and Queen Elinor. They had triplet sons who were mischief-makers, and a head-strong daughter, called Merida.

Every day, Queen Elinor spent hour after hour teaching Merida how a princess should behave. Merida refused to listen. She preferred to have play sword fights with her father.

Sometimes, the queen wondered how she would ever get through to her daughter.

Merida dreaded her mother's lessons. They were so boring! Her favourite thing to do was to ride her horse, Angus, through the forests of DunBroch, practising with her bow and arrows. Merida was a brilliant archer and hardly ever missed a shot.

One day, Queen Elinor told her daughter it was time to follow family tradition and invite the sons of the Highland clan lords to compete for the princess's hand in marriage. But Merida said she wasn't ready to marry!

Queen Elinor told her a legend about an ancient prince who had refused to follow the traditions of his kingdom. He had split from his three brothers and their kingdom had fallen.

"Legends are lessons," said the queen. Merida didn't agree.

Unfortunately for Merida, the clans were
already on their way! A few days later, the royal
family welcomed them into the castle's Great Hall.
The three lords stepped forward to greet the
DunBroch clan.

Young Macintosh was the first to be introduced.

"With his own sword, he defeated *one thousand* foes!" his father, Lord Macintosh, bragged.

Next, was Young MacGuffin. "With his bare hands, he defeated *two thousand* foes!" his father, Lord MacGuffin, boasted.

Wee Dingwall was last. "He defeated *ten thousand* foes single-handedly!" his father, Lord Dingwall, bluffed.

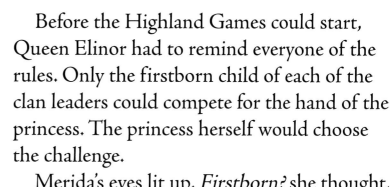

Before the Highland Games could start, Queen Elinor had to remind everyone of the rules. Only the firstborn child of each of the clan leaders could compete for the hand of the princess. The princess herself would choose the challenge.

Merida's eyes lit up. *Firstborn?* she thought. Suddenly, she had an idea.

"I choose archery!" she cried.

The competition took place on the castle grounds that very afternoon. Young MacGuffin almost missed his target altogether.

Young Macintosh's shot was better – but his attitude was not.

Wee Dingwall was the worst archer of all. But, somehow, he managed to hit the bullseye!

Then Merida appeared on the field.

"I am the firstborn child of Clan DunBroch!" she declared. "And I'll be shooting for my own hand!"

"I forbid it!" Queen Elinor cried. Merida ignored her mother and aimed her first arrow towards the target.

One … two … three arrows took flight and
each arrow hit the bullseye on all three targets!
Merida was thrilled, until a furious Queen
Elinor dragged her back into the castle.

"You embarrassed them!" the queen shouted at Merida when they were alone. "You embarrassed me!"

"I'll never be like you!" Merida cried, angrily. She slashed the family tapestry with a sword, splitting the images of of her and her mother.

Merida ran out of the castle. Sobbing, she jumped on her horse and raced into the forest.

Soon, she arrived at the mysterious Ring of Stones. Tiny blue lights appeared and formed a trail. They seemed to be beckoning Merida to go deeper into the forest.

The blue lights were will o' the wisps. These
playful spirits were known for leading people either
to their treasure or to their doom!
Merida followed the wisps to a small, old cottage
deep in the woods, where an old woman lived.

Merida believed that the old
woman was a witch. So, she asked
for a spell that would change her
mother's mind about her marriage.

"Long ago, I met a prince," the Witch told Merida.
The prince had given the Witch a ring engraved with
two axes in exchange for a spell that would give him the
strength of ten men.

The Witch set to work casting the spell. When she had finished, she pulled a cake from her cauldron and gave it to Merida.

Since she had done as Merida had asked, the Witch asked her to leave. The Witch just wanted to be left in peace! So, Merida headed home with the spell cake....

At the castle, Elinor was happy and relieved to see Merida. The lords were still expecting an answer. Which son would the princess choose to marry?

Merida handed her mother the cake. "I made it," she said, excitedly. "For you!"

After one bite of cake, the queen put her fork down.
She suggested that they go and settle things with the lords.
Soon, the queen began to feel ill. Was the spell taking
effect? Dodging King Fergus and the lords, Merida led her
mother up to her room.

Queen Elinor went straight to bed.
After a few minutes, a giant bear rose from the sheets.
The queen had been transformed into a bear!
"That scaffy witch gave me a gammy spell!" Merida cried.
Elinor-Bear let out an angry roar!

Downstairs, King Fergus heard the bear roar.
Long ago, the king had lost one of his legs to
an evil bear called Mor'du. Ever since, the king
had hunted down every bear he'd come across.
Now, there was a bear in his castle! King
Fergus quickly gathered all the clans for a hunt.

Merida knew she had to find the Witch so that she could undo the spell. She asked her brothers to distract the king so that she and her mother could slip out of the castle.

The triplets used a chicken to cast the shadow of a bear onto the wall. When the king saw it, he took off after the bear, leading the hunting party in the wrong direction. Merida and her mother quickly headed for the woods.

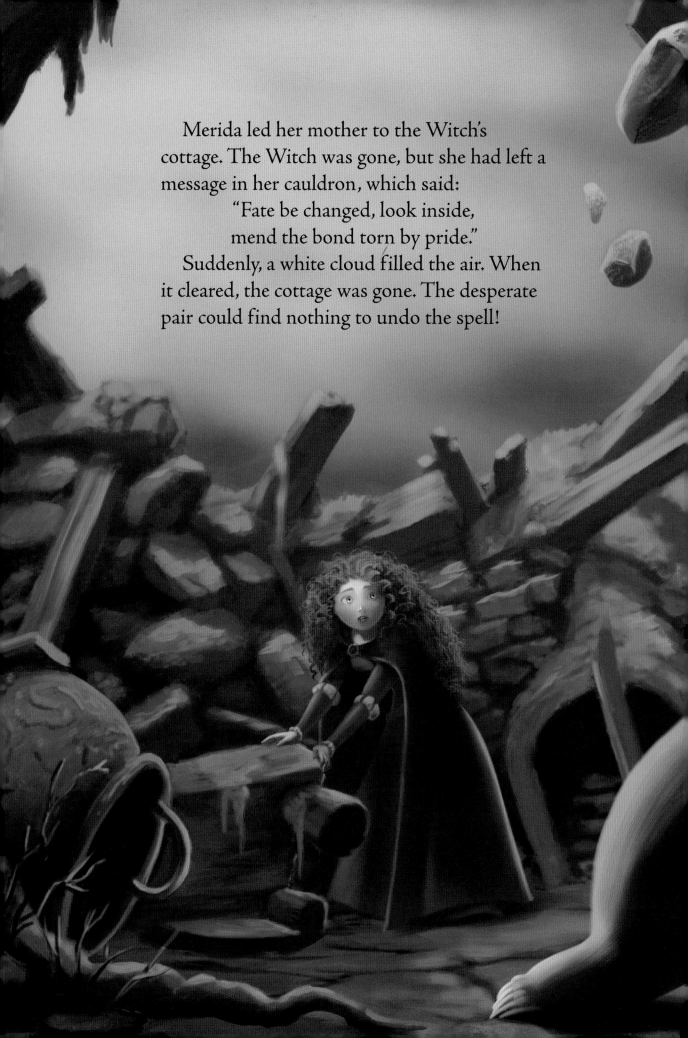

Merida led her mother to the Witch's cottage. The Witch was gone, but she had left a message in her cauldron, which said:
"Fate be changed, look inside,
mend the bond torn by pride."
Suddenly, a white cloud filled the air. When it cleared, the cottage was gone. The desperate pair could find nothing to undo the spell!

Merida and her mother spent the night in the
forest. In the morning, Elinor picked some berries for
breakfast and sat down to her queenly meal.
    Merida decided to get them a *real* breakfast.

In a nearby stream, Merida showed Elinor how to catch fish and together they played and splashed in the river. For the first time in a long while, mother and daughter enjoyed each other's company.

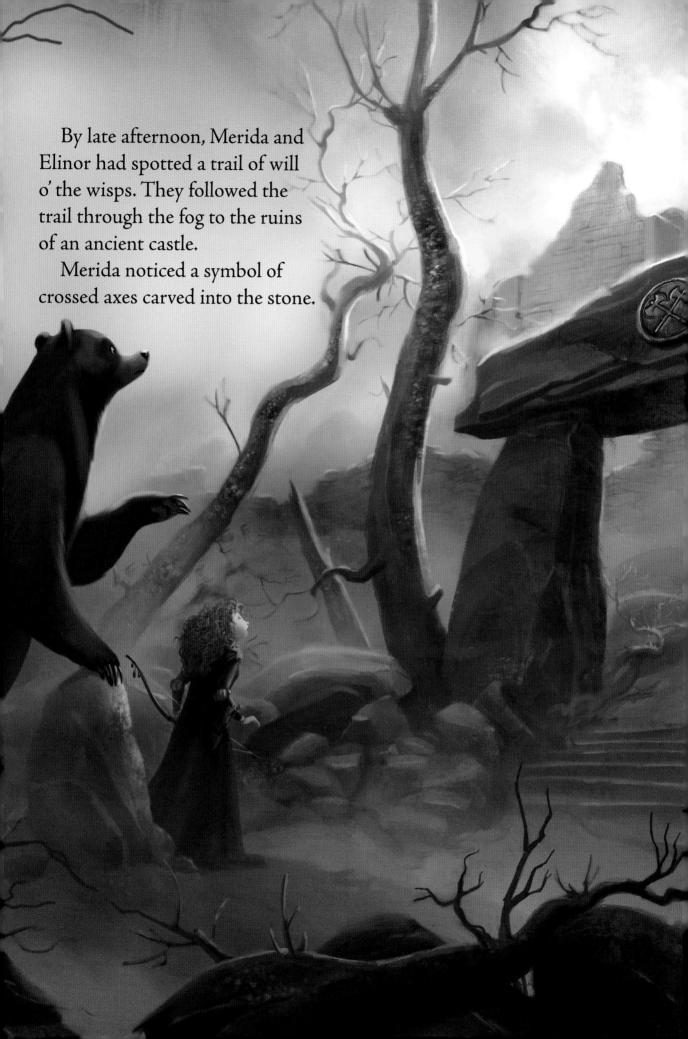

By late afternoon, Merida and
Elinor had spotted a trail of will
o' the wisps. They followed the
trail through the fog to the ruins
of an ancient castle.

Merida noticed a symbol of
crossed axes carved into the stone.

As they looked around the ruins, Merida tumbled into the castle's throne room. There she saw a stone carving of four brothers – all of them were princes – but the fourth brother was broken off. It was just like her mother's legend.

"Split," Merida whispered, "like the tapestry."

Merida noticed deep claw marks
throughout the room.

"The strength of ten men," Merida
said, remembering the Witch's words
and the prince's ring with the crossed
axes. "The prince became ... Mor'du!"
Just then, Mor'du appeared!

Mor'du lunged at Merida, but the queen pulled the princess out of his reach just in time. Merida and her mother raced away from the ruined castle.

Back at the Ring of Stones, Merida suddenly remembered the Witch's message: "mend the bond torn by pride". She realized that to break the spell, she had to return to the castle and mend the family tapestry that she had torn! Mother and daughter headed home as fast as they could.

Merida sneaked her mother into the Great Hall. The clans were brawling over Merida! Elinor-Bear hid in the shadows, posing as a stuffed bear and coached her daughter through her speech.

Merida announced, "The queen feels in her heart … that we should be free to follow our own hearts … and find love in our own time."

Moved by Merida's words, the young lords decided that they wanted to be able to choose their own fates, too. "That settles it!" said Lord MacGuffin. The lords agreed that Merida and the young men should be free to marry for love.

As soon as they could, Merida and her mother raced upstairs to get the tapestry.

Just after they entered the room, Fergus burst in – and saw the bear!

"Dad, no!" Merida cried. "It's not what you think!"

The king swung his sword. Elinor-Bear ran out of the door and down the hallway. The clans chased her as she tried to escape from the castle.

Merida tried to explain to her father what had happened, but Fergus didn't believe her. He locked Merida in the Tapestry Room to keep her safe. Then he raced off to hunt the bear.

Meanwhile, the triplets had eaten the spell cake and become bears, too! Now, Merida had to fix the tapestry to save her mother and her brothers.

After the triplets freed their sister from the tapestry room, they all climbed onto Angus and raced after their mother. All the while, Merida mended the tapestry.

Merida found the hunters at the Ring of Stones. The men had captured Elinor. "I won't let you kill my mother!" Merida cried. She swung her sword at King Fergus's wooden leg, chopping it clean off!

Suddenly, Mor'du burst into the
Ring of Stones. The clans rushed
to attack him, but they were no
match for the beast.

Mor'du quickly closed in on Merida.

Determined to protect her
daughter, Elinor gathered her
strength and broke free.
Then she charged at Mor'du.

The two bears clashed. After a fierce battle,
Elinor slammed Mor'du against a standing stone.
The great rock broke apart, crushing Mor'du.

The battle won, Merida wrapped the mended
tapestry around Elinor-Bear. But nothing happened.
"I don't care what you are," she cried. "You're
still my mum. I love you." Merida buried her face in
Elinor's fur and wept as dawn began to break.

As she wept, Merida felt a hand stroke her hair. She looked up. Her mother, back to her old self, was smiling down at her. The bond between them had been repaired. The spell was broken.

Soon Merida and Queen Elinor were spending more time together and enjoying each other's company. The queen knew Merida would marry someday, but not until she was ready. And Merida knew that she didn't want to change anything about her mother. She loved her mum just the way she was.

The End